Freddy the Frogcaster™ and the Flash Flood

By JANICE DEAN "The Weather Machine"

Illustrated by RUSS COX

Freddy the Frogcaster™ and Regnery Kids™ are trademarks of Salem Communications Holding Corporation; Regnery® is a registered trademark of Salem Communications Holding Corporation

Weather-Ready Nation Ambassador™ and the Weather-Ready Nation Ambassador™ logo are trademarks of the U.S. Department of Commerce, National Oceanic and Atmospheric Administration, used with permission.

Cataloging-in-Publication data on file with the Library of Congress

ISBN 978-1-62157-470-5

Published in the United States by
Regnery Kids
An imprint of Regnery Publishing
300 New Jersey Avenue NW
Washington, DC 20001
www.RegneryKids.com

Manufactured in the United States of America

10 9 8 7 6 5 4 3 2 1

Books are available in quantity for promotional or premium use. For information on discounts and terms, please visit our website: www.Regnery.com.

Distributed to the trade by
Perseus Distribution
www.perseusdistribution.com

To my sweet tadpoles, Matthew and Theodore.
My heart leaps for joy when I'm with you.

Freddy the Frogcaster is your Weather-Ready Nation Ambassador™,
a program of the National Oceanic and Atmospheric Administration (NOAA)

Freddy the Frogcaster was busy preparing his weather report at the Frog News Network. Freddy's fellow frogcasters Sally Croaker and Polly Woggins had given him more and more responsibility, and now he was officially a weekend weather reporter!

Freddy just loved thinking, talking, and learning about all kinds of weather, and the whole town of Lilypad trusted and listened to Freddy's frogcasting.

Freddy hopped outside to take a break and check out some weather clues. Would it be another day without rain? Lilypad was having a drought and it was starting to affect their neighborhood.

The plants and grass were brown and wilted.
Looking out, Freddy noticed some dark clouds
in the distance.

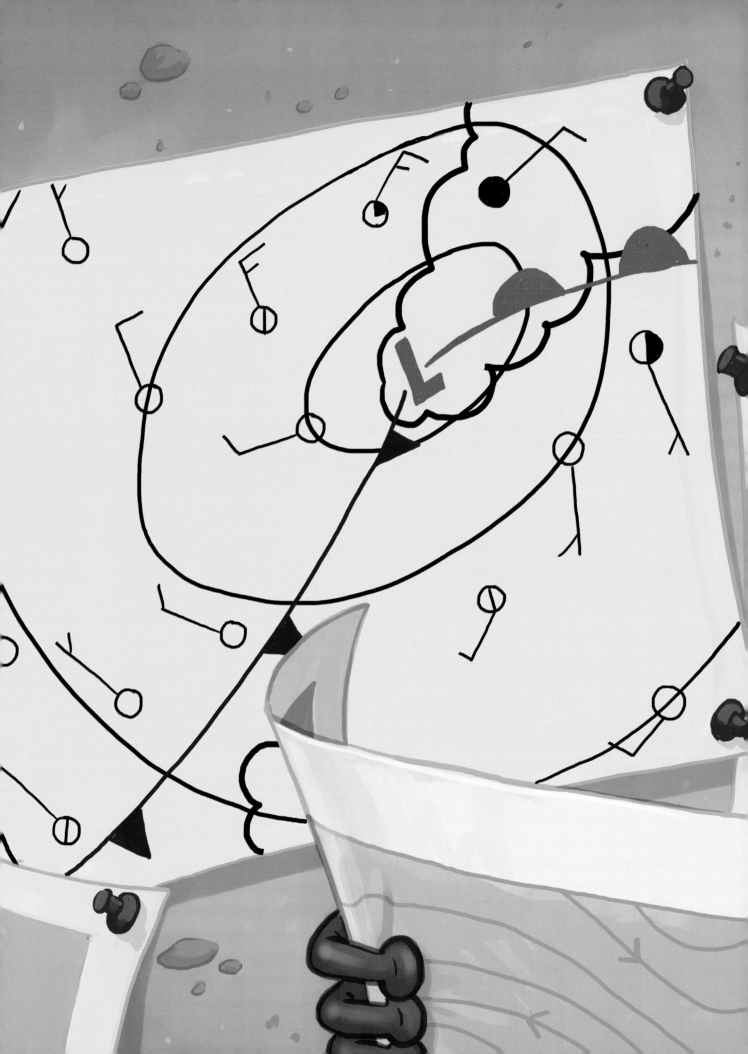

He ran back inside to look at his weather tools and charts. A storm to the west of Lilypad could bring some much-needed rain. He looked at the winds, the temperature, and the position of the jet stream on his maps. Yes, indeed there was a storm on the way!

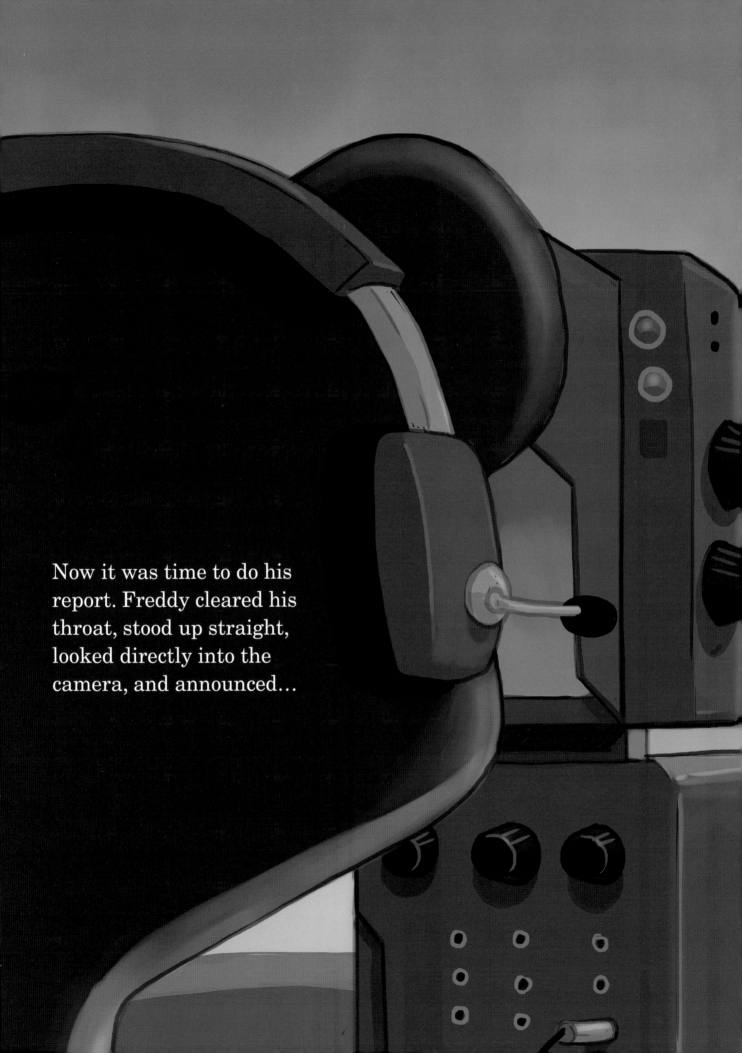

Now it was time to do his report. Freddy cleared his throat, stood up straight, looked directly into the camera, and announced...

"Hello, everyone. I'm Freddy the Frogcaster. A storm is coming, possibly bringing lots of rain. And because the ground is so dry, it's going to be hard for it to soak up all the water. A flash flood watch is up for our area and it doesn't take much water to knock a frog off its feet or to carry a frogcar downstream. Time to get prepared."

Back home, Freddy took another look at his weather maps and charts. The radar showed the storm right on track to be near Lilypad tomorrow afternoon.

The next day the clouds began to roll in and a few raindrops fell…but that was it! Freddy looked at his weather app on his phone. Oh no! The rain had moved to the north of them. Freddy had gotten his report wrong.

"When is the rain coming?" Freddy's friends asked.

"Uhhh. Well…um. It isn't coming," Freddy announced.

"What do you mean the rain isn't coming? All our after-school sports were canceled! You said we might have a flood or even a flash flood."

Freddy's face started to get hot and he felt a big lump in his throat.

"You know…weather frogcasting is not an exact science. Sometimes we get the frogcast wrong. But it's always good to be prepared."

One of the kids cracked, "Your nickname should be False-Alarm Freddy!" Freddy turned his head and tried not to cry.

That night Freddy was so upset he couldn't eat his dinner. He told his parents about being teased at school.

"Freddy, you did your best. You studied your charts and made your report. Can you imagine if you hadn't warned them and Lilypad got flooded and no one was prepared? You did the right thing!" said his dad.

Freddy still felt terrible. All he could think of was False-Alarm Freddy.

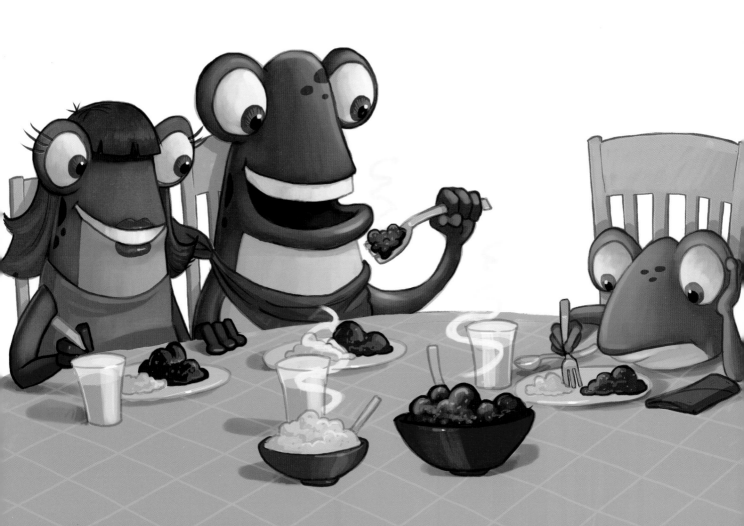

Just then he got a call from Sally and Polly.
"Please don't fret, Freddy," Polly pleaded.
"There's always a chance the weather doesn't
happen the way we think it's going to."

Sally agreed, "There have been many frogcasts
that I have gotten wrong. But it's better to be
prepared than caught in a bad storm without
warning." Freddy felt a little better. He knew
in his heart he couldn't give up his dreams of
being a frogcaster.

Frog News Alert...... Frog

Freddy returned to work, but he was very nervous because he saw another storm coming and the rain totals looked even bigger. Gulp. Freddy began his weather update and hoped everyone would listen.

"Remember, fellow frogs, if flooding happens, go to higher ground and don't try to walk across flowing streams or drive through flooded roadways. If water rises in your home before you evacuate, go to the top floor, attic, or roof. Listen to your NOAA weather radio for the latest storm information and please be weather ready!" pleaded Freddy.

News Alert...... Frog News

The next day, the rain came just like Freddy had predicted. He could see out his window that this was a dangerous situation. Freddy tried to make his way to the TV station, but the water was too high and he didn't want to get stranded.

He would take his own advice and stay indoors.

Trees fell, and floodwater gushed out over the streams and river banks causing cars to be swept away.

Sally was out reporting near Freddy's house on all the water rescues happening around Lilypad.

Police and firefrogs were out trying to help those who were caught in the rushing water. This was a bad situation.

Flood reports kept coming in. Freddy knew that flash floods could cause more damage than hurricanes, tornadoes, wind storms, or lightning. He watched Polly interview rescue workers that had just saved a mother and her babies from floodwaters. Thankfully, they were okay.

The next day the rain finally ended and the waters started to go down.

"It turned out that this storm stalled over Lilypad and we received over a foot of rain in just six hours. That's another record for Lilypad!" Sally reported.

Later that day, the mayor announced it was safe for everyone to come out. He thanked all the police and firefrogs who helped with the rescues. "This was a big flood and it caused a lot of damage to our little town, but thankfully everyone is safe. And a special thanks to our favorite frogcasters, Sally, Polly, and Freddy… for getting this last frogcast right and warning us of the potential rain and flooding," the mayor said.

Sally and Polly hugged Freddy. "Don't be scared to take chances. There will be times that we get our frogcasting wrong. Weather is unpredictable that way. We do our best to warn everyone about the weather with the information we have at the time. Just remember, you will always be Weather-Ready Freddy to us!"

Freddy loved it when Sally and Polly called him Weather-Ready Freddy.

Just then, Freddy looked up and saw a dark cloud in the distance. He'd better get going. It looked like another storm was headed their way. Time for this frogcaster to do what he did best. He couldn't waste another moment—and hopped to it!

Hi, Friends!

Rain gets a bad rap sometimes. It's actually one of the most important things on earth. It gives us water to drink, helps farmers grow crops, and keeps everything green. Too little rain can cause a drought like the one we had in Lilypad. Too much rain can cause big problems. Did you know flooding causes more damage in the United States than any other severe weather-related event? It's true and that's why it's important to be prepared when it comes to flooding and flash flooding.

What is a flood?

There are many ways in which a flood can happen: thunderstorms can bring flooding rainfall; storms from the ocean (hurricanes) can cause water to pile up onto land and cause floods; or flooding can happen when a dam breaks or jammed ice backs up water flow. Believe it or not, floods are the most expensive natural disaster, causing millions of dollars of damage a year.

Thankfully, forecasters (meteorologists) can help predict where the worst of the flooding might be and people can prepare in advance. But other times flooding can happen very quickly without much notice.

Many people aren't prepared when a flood occurs.

Walking through water where you can't see the ground can knock you off your feet. Just six inches of rapidly moving flood water can knock a person down.

Nearly eighty percent of flash flood deaths are auto related. Just two feet of water can float a large vehicle or even a bus and carry it away! This is why you should never drive through flooded roads.

The most common type of flood is from rivers. If there is more water than the river can hold, then water overflows along the banks and affects surrounding areas. Waves from the ocean can cause flooding—from weather systems like hurricanes or a large wave from a tsunami. Sites close to the ocean or near rivers are more prone to flooding events.

Flash flood facts:

Flash floods are the number one weather-related killer in the United States. Flash flooding is an extreme version of flooding. It can happen very quickly without a lot of warning. In *Freddy the Frogcaster and the Flash Flood*, Lilypad was having a drought (dry land without a lot of rain for a long period of time) and the ground became very hard—and as a result the rain didn't soak into the ground.

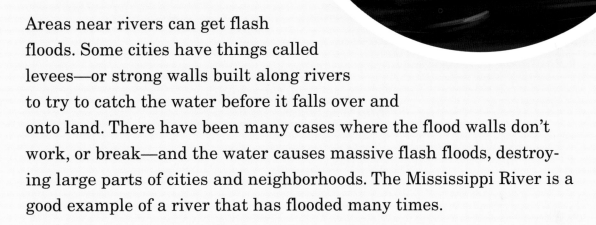

In cities and towns where a lot of people live, buildings, streets, sidewalks, highways, and parking lots can be very prone to floods because the water can't be absorbed into concrete.

Areas near rivers can get flash floods. Some cities have things called levees—or strong walls built along rivers to try to catch the water before it falls over and onto land. There have been many cases where the flood walls don't work, or break—and the water causes massive flash floods, destroying large parts of cities and neighborhoods. The Mississippi River is a good example of a river that has flooded many times.

Mountains and hill areas are prone to flash flooding. Rocks and clay soil on a mountain can't absorb water very well, so it can flow down the mountain side like a slide! In the springtime, melting snow can also add water to the streams and cause them to overflow.

Flash flooding can occur in frozen areas when ice begins to melt or in situations where large chunks of ice get jammed up and water rises behind it, creating an ice jam.

Dam breaks can also cause major flash flooding with deadly consequences. In 1889 a dam break in Johnstown, Pennsylvania released a thirty- to forty-foot wall of water that killed 2,000 people in minutes.

How do people (and frogs!) know when flooding is possible?

Local news shows, radio shows, and the Internet help spread the word. Here's what those advisories mean:

FLOOD WATCH—means that there is a possibility that flooding will occur in a specified area over a period longer than six hours.

FLASH FLOOD WATCH—means that flash flooding is possible in or close to the watch area. Flash Flood Watches can be put into effect for as long as twelve hours, while heavy rains move into and across the area.

FLOOD WARNING—means that flooding conditions are actually occurring in the warning area.

FLASH FLOOD WARNING—means that flash flooding is actually occurring in the warning area. A warning can also be issued as a result of torrential rains, a dam failure, or snow thaw.

FLOOD WATCH

Get ready in the next 24-48 hours for heavy rainfall in the area that could result in flash flooding. It is very difficult to pinpoint exactly where flooding will develop so you'll want to pay close attention to forecast updates.

FLOOD ADVISORY

Flooding that may not necessarily be life threatening but could cause impacts to travel and potentially become dangerous. Slick roadways, hydroplaning, standing water over roadways, and a few low water crossing closures are all possibilities in an advisory.

FLOOD WARNING

Flash flooding is either imminent or already ongoing. Many times, flash flooding has been reported within the warning area and conditions are expected to worsen, and potentially rapidly.

How can you BE PREPARED for a flood?

BE WEATHER READY!: Have a disaster plan and prepare a disaster supplies kit for your home and car. Include a first aid kit, canned food, can opener, bottled water, battery-operated radio, flashlight, protective clothing, and written instructions on how to turn off electricity, gas, and water.

DURING A FLOOD: Move to a safe area quickly. Move to higher ground, like the highest floor of your home. Avoid areas subject to sudden flooding like low spots and canyons. Avoid already flooded areas. If a flowing stream of water is above your ankles, stop, turn around, and go the other way. Do not attempt to drive through a flooded road. The depth of the water is not obvious and the road may be washed away. If your car stalls, leave it and seek higher ground. Rapidly rising water may engulf the car and pick it up and sweep it away. Kids should never play around high water, storm drains, or viaducts. Be cautious at night, because its harder to see flood dangers. If told to evacuate, do so immediately.

What were some of the worst floods in U.S. history?

The worst flood in U.S. history resulted from a dam break upstream from Johnstown, Pennsylvania, on May 31, 1889. Although ample warnings were given, they were disregarded by many townspeople, and 2,200 residents died.

Hurricane Katrina, a Category 4 hurricane along the eastern Louisiana-western Mississippi coastlines in August 2005, resulted in severe storm surge damage (maximum surge probably exceeded twenty-five feet) along the Louisiana-Mississippi-Alabama coasts, wind damage, and the failure of parts of the levee system in New Orleans. Inland effects included high winds and some flooding in the states of Alabama, Mississippi, Florida, Tennessee, Kentucky, Indiana, Ohio, and Georgia. Preliminary estimates were well over $100 billion in damages/costs and more than 1,200 fatalities.

On February 26, 1972, the Buffalo Creek Dam located in southern West Virginia collapsed, sending a black wave of water through one coal mining town after another, and killing more than a hundred people. Four thousand people were left homeless.

On July 31, 1976, a storm in northern Colorado dumped a foot of rain into the Big Thompson Canyon, producing a raging torrent of water nineteen feet high, and resulting in 145 deaths.

A note from Janice about frogcasting/forecasting: *In Freddy the Frogcaster and the Flash Flood,* Freddy got his forecast wrong! Freddy was hurt when his friends called him False-Alarm Freddy. That sometimes happens to meteorologists like me when, occasionally, viewers will write mean emails or tweets if our forecast is wrong. Take it from Janice Dean "The Weather Machine": We would much rather have everyone prepared for a big weather event even if the forecast doesn't turn out as we predicted.

The best weather forecasts in the world are made in the United States, but there's always room for error. Thankfully, meteorologists are getting better and better at predicting storms with advanced technology and forecasting tools (computer models/maps/satellite) that help predict where flooding can happen. Unfortunately, mother nature doesn't always cooperate! When our predictions are wrong, we try to learn from our mistakes and will continue to warn our community to be prepared for dangerous weather.

How can I find out if I am in danger from a flood?

NOAA Weather Radio All Hazards is one of the best ways to receive warnings from the National Weather Service. NOAA Weather Radio All Hazards is a nationwide network of radio stations broadcasting continuous weather and river information direct from nearby NWS offices. Also, the NWS website provides forecasts and warnings, and identifies where flooding is occurring.

Stay safe, friends!

Freddy the Frogcaster

Acknowledgments

To Sean. Together we can weather any storm. Thank you for our family.

To Russ Cox—the best illustrator a girl could ever ask for. Thank you for keeping Lilypad vibrant and exciting.

To Cheryl and Peter Barnes for nurturing and encouraging my Freddy idea.

To Brandon Noriega for your calm and measured forecasting and your keen eye on Freddy's frogcasts.

To my support team at Regnery Kids—Cheryl Barnes, Marji Ross, Mark Bloomfield, Nancy Feuerborn, and Emily Beasley.

To Doug Brunt for the brilliant False-Alarm Freddy idea—and your forgiveness about a bad beach forecast.

To Megyn Kelly. I'm a better person, mom, and friend because of you.

To Shannon Bream and your wonderful "shannonigans."

To my *Fox & Friends* family for making mornings fun again. To Lauren Petterson and Gavin Hadden for letting me dance.

To Dianne Brandi for also cheering on Freddy.

To all the kidcasters out there who have read Freddy and are now weather ready. You're frogtastic!

To my mom, Stella, for always being there for me and my family.

Enjoy more of Freddy's weather adventures in

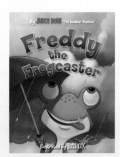   

978-1-62157-084-4   978-1-62157-254-1   978-1-62157-260-2   978-1-62157-469-9